Eleven Turtle Tales

Eleven Turtle Tales

Adventure Tales from
Around the World

PLEASANT DESPAIN

ILLUSTRATIONS BY JOE SHLICHTA

A   nc.
L   K

Printed in the United States of America

10 9 8 7 6 5 4 3 2 1

ISBN 0-87483-388-4 (HB) $12.95
LC# 94-23093

Executive editor: Liz Parkhurst
Project editor: Rufus Griscom
Design director: Ted Parkhurst
Cover design: Harvill-Ross Studios, Ltd.
Cover illustration: Joe Shlichta
Illustrations: Joe Shlichta

The paper used in this publication meets the minimum requirements of
the American National Standard for Information Sciences—Permanence of
Paper for Printed Library Materials, ANSI Z39.48-1984.

AUGUST HOUSE, INC.   PUBLISHERS   LITTLE ROCK

For T.R. Welch,

Master gardener
True friend

Contents

Acknowledgments

A completed book is always
a collaborative affair.
Heartfelt thanks to:

Leslie Gillian Abel
Joe Shlichta
Tony Earl
Rufus Griscom
Liz Parkhurst
Ted Parkhurst

and the good people of the
Seattle Public Library who gave me use of
the C.K. Poe Fratt Writers' Room,
the room in which most of these tales
were finally written down.

Rise up, my love, my fair one, and come away.

For, lo! the winter is past, the rain is over and gone;

The flowers appear on the earth;

The time of the singing of birds is come,

And the voice of the turtle is heard in our land.

The Song of Solomon

Ecclesiastes. XII, 10-12.

Introduction

Turtle carries the world on her back. The story is told in myth, legend, and poem. It is found in the ancient stories of the East and in the more current tales of the West. Storytellers of indigenous peoples have passed it on for centuries. Contemporary tellers from all over the world continue to share it today.

Turtle carries the world on her back—the image is rich with symbolism. We are reminded that the planet upon which we walk is an ancient and living thing. Both Turtle and earth are unhurried and wise, eternal and forgiving.

Turtle swims in water, walks on land, and breathes air: she joins three of the four elements of creation into one. She is the symbol of mother Earth; she is Turtle Island, the grounded aspect of life. We would do well to learn from Turtle.

Over the many years and thousands of miles that I've traveled to schools and storytelling events, I've often carried a symbol of Turtle with me. When asked "Why? What is the significance?" I've always told the same story. Turtle carries our world on her back, and with it, our stories. Our stories come from our lives, even when we make them up. Turtle reminds us of the *source* of our stories. And when we remember the source, we tend to speak more truthfully.

I've chosen the tales in this collection for several reasons. First and foremost, they are tellable. Second, they are from many cultures. Third, they show Turtle in a variety of roles, from helper to trickster to advisor. Hopefully,

they will delight you and your listeners and
teach you about the many masks Turtle so
effortlessly wears.

Enjoy!

Pleasant DeSpain
Seattle, Washington
January, 1994

Why California Has Earthquakes

Native American (Gabrielino)

Long, long before there was a land called California, the entire surface of the earth was covered with water. It was a quiet and lonely place.

One morning, Great Spirit looked upon the earth and said, "I want company. I'll make some land." He looked all about and saw water everywhere. "Now what will I use to hold up this land?" he asked.

Suddenly a great sea turtle, whose green shell was as large as an island, swam by. Great Spirit called to Turtle and asked how many brothers and sisters he had.

"Three brothers and three sisters," answered

Turtle.

"Are they all as big as you?" asked Great Spirit.

"Oh yes," said turtle. "Some are even bigger."

"Call your brothers and sisters together and bring them to me. I want to talk to all of you at one time," Great Spirit ordered.

Turtle swam slowly to the West in search of his family. It took him the entire first day to find his oldest sister. On the second day he met up with his youngest brother. On the third day he bumped into his twin. All in all, six days were required to find all six of his sisters and brothers. On the seventh day, they swam together to Great Spirit. He was pleased when he saw the seven islands floating together as one. *Yes, he said to himself, I will have land after all.*

Great Spirit asked the turtle family to line up, oldest to youngest, head to tail, and north to south. They agreed, and formed a straight line, the oldest son at the northernmost tip and the youngest daughter at the southernmost point. "No," said Great Spirit, "it doesn't look quite right. I want the three youngest turtles at the southern end to shift to the east, just a bit."

The turtles obeyed and Great Spirit was satisfied. "Stay perfectly still," he said to the turtles. "It is now your job to hold up the land that will one day be called California. It is a great privilege and you will long be praised."

The turtles were happy to be so honored and remained still and calm as Great Spirit began to pull wet, goopy mud and sand from the ocean's floor and plaster it on their backs. He packed on layer after layer, fusing them into one long, gigantic island. The jagged tops of the turtle family's hard shells rose high into the air, far above the newly-made land. Great Spirit said, "I'll leave them as they are. They will make majestic mountain ranges."

Great Spirit decided to plant trees on the

northern half of the land, and leave sandy soil on the southern half. He used his strong thumb and long fingers to punch deep holes and dig long troughs into the new earth for lakes, rivers and streams. He made certain that all the fresh water flowed to the west in order to run off into the salty sea.

Then Great Spirit made the birds to sing and the animals to run, the wind to blow and the clouds to rain. When he had finished, he was pleased.

Then came trouble. The turtle family had grown restless sitting so still for so long. They wanted to go for a swim in the big ocean. The four brothers decided to swim in a westerly direction to watch the setting of the sun. The three sisters wanted to swim in an easterly direction to watch the sun rise. They argued with each other for several hours and couldn't come to an agreement. The brothers stopped arguing and began to swim toward the west. The sisters stopped arguing and began to swim toward the east.

KA-BOOM! The new land cracked and split in two! The island rumbled and shook and roared! The split zigzagged and widened and smoked and sped from one end of the land to the other. Just as suddenly as it began, the earth-grinding ceased. The turtles were stopped short and the island stood still. For the many layers of mud had dried hard on their backs and they had become fused as one. The turtles made peace with each other, knowing that they would be together for a long time to come.

Even in the best of families, however, brothers and sisters grow weary of each other and want to separate, if only for a brief time. And each time Turtle Family argues, the land that is called California cracks and shakes and roars. Trees and dwellings fall down, and the animals and birds, and humans too, fear for their lives. Then the turtles forgive each other and the land knows peace and calm once again.

The Courting of Miss Python

Central Africa (Congo)

M iss Python was the most beautiful snake in the forest. Her long, graceful body glistened in the sunlight. Her dark, slitted eyes were full of mystery. Her sharp, flickering fangs were hypnotic. She was *so* beautiful that all the male reptiles, animals, and birds who were yet unmarried wanted her for a wife.

Miss Python was also of the age to marry, and she had secretly fallen in love with Turtle. She asked him to run away with her.

Turtle said, "No, we should wait for the proper time and ask your father for permission to wed."

Miss Python's father, however, was the King

of Pythons, and he was as brutal as she was lovely. All the creatures of the forest feared his cold-blooded grip of death. And King Python decided that none of the forest creatures would ever be worthy of his daughter.

One day Elephant, the largest animal in the forest, decided that he wanted to marry Miss Python. He stomped and crashed through the trees causing the ground to shake. Then he lifted his massive trunk high into the air and trumpeted loudly.

King Python crawled out of his hole in the rocks, angry that his afternoon nap had been disturbed. He focused his piercing eyes on Elephant, and Elephant's skin began to crawl. Fearing Python's strangle hold, Elephant turned and ran back into the forest, trampling trees in his flight.

Cheetah, the fastest land animal, boasted of his bravery and said that he would marry Miss

Python. He ran to King Python's home in the rocks and circled around it so fast that he created a small cyclone. Python was eating his dinner and became angry at having his meal so rudely interrupted. He slithered up and out of the ground to face the whirling cat. Python's massive mouth opened wide, ready to swallow and crunch Cheetah. Using his powerful hind legs, Cheetah leaped high into the air, fleeing certain death.

Brilliantly-colored Parrot said that he was a sweet-talker, and that he could surely win King Python's friendship. "Then," he explained, "I'll ask to marry Miss Python."

He flew to the rocky ledge, and began to squawk and sing in his loudest voice. King Python was daydreaming and became quite irritated at the disturbance. He snaked out of the hole and unwound his entire length. Parrot screamed and flew right back into the forest.

Finally Turtle, compact and bold, decided it was time to wed. He crawled slowly and quietly to the rocky hillside and spoke to King Python. "I am Turtle, here to marry your lovely daughter, if you please."

Python slithered out of his hole, and with his long and powerful body, surrounded Turtle. He smiled cruelly at the small suitor and said, "Let me embrace you and welcome you to our family." The snake wound round and round Turtle, coil upon coil, and then began to squeeze.

Turtle felt himself being crunched and quickly ducked his head and pulled his legs into his hard shell. Python squeezed and strangled until he was sure Turtle was dead. Then he uncoiled his heavy body and began to slither away.

But Turtle wasn't dead. He wasn't even hurt. Out popped his head from his shell, and with a smile he said, "Thanks for the big hug, friend Python. Now I feel welcomed to the family."

There was fire in King Python's eyes as he snarled, "Now I'll give you a little toss. It's a family ritual." He grabbed Turtle's shell with his teeth and threw him high into the air. "He'll crack in half when he lands," laughed Python. "It's just what he deserves for being so bold."

Turtle enjoyed the ride on the way up. He ducked into his shell for the return to earth, and bounced three times upon the ground. He came out of his shell and said, "What a fun trip! I've never before traveled so high and fast! You are a good friend, Python."

"If I can't crush Turtle, and if I can't break him, then I'll have to eat him," said the snake, and he opened his massive mouth wide and swallowed him with one gulp! Down, down the slippery slope Turtle traveled, all the way to Python's stomach. Of course he tucked his head and legs inside for the journey. Once inside the dark stomach Turtle poked his four legs out of his shell. Then he tickled Python from deep inside.

King Python had never felt anything like the funny stomach ache he was having and began to laugh and burp at the same time. He laughed and burped and burped and laughed, and Turtle was slowly forced back up the long tunnel. With the final loud burp, Turtle flew out of Python's mouth and onto the grass.

"Thank you, King Python!" said Turtle. "That was the most fun I've had all day. I'm so pleased that you will be my father-in-law."

Python was perplexed. "If I can't crush him, and if I can't break him in two, and if I can't swallow him, then there is only one thing left to do, and that is ..."

"Yes, Father?" asked Miss Python as she slid out from the hole in the rocks.

"Yes, Father-in-law-to-be?" asked Turtle.

"Marry them," said King Python.

"Yes!" shouted Miss Python and Turtle in unison.

And so it happened that upon the following afternoon, with all the forest creatures present, Turtle and Miss Python became husband and wife.

The Talkative King

India

L ong ago in India, a large, old tortoise dreamed of flying through the air like a bird.

Long ago in India, a talkative king decided to celebrate his royal birthday by giving a five-hour speech to his subjects.

"Now, what," you ask, "does the king have to do with the tortoise?"

Keep reading, and you will find out.

The tortoise lived in a beautiful pond at the base of the Himalayas. She was friend to fish, frog, and fowl, and everyone spoke kindly of her. The only time her temper flared was if someone kidded her for walking so slowly.

"I'm slow but steady," was her usual reply.

"And you have a rude mouth."

One day the tortoise asked two wild geese to take her flying with them. "I wish to see the earth from high above," she explained.

"But you have no feathers," said the birds. "How can you fly?"

"I've been thinking about it for some time," explained the tortoise, "and I believe I've discovered a possible method. Find a strong stick that you can hold at each end with your beaks. I'll bite it in the middle, and you can fly away together and carry me aloft."

"You would have to bite very hard and keep your mouth closed the whole time," said one of the geese.

"I know," said the tortoise. "I've thought it all through."

The birds found a proper stick, and with the tortoise biting its center, took off in flight. They flew fast and high and soon were sailing over the mountain tops. The tortoise, both frightened and exhilarated, swayed in the air. It was the adventure of her lifetime!

Soon they flew over the city of Benares. Several children were outdoors at play and looked up into the sky.

"Look!" said a clever boy, "Mistress Tortoise is chasing the geese through the sky. But at that slow pace, she'll never catch them!"

Tortoise heard the comment from below and became quite angry. She couldn't help herself and opened her mouth to say, "I'm slow but steady, and you have a rude mouth," and down, down, down she fell, right into the courtyard pond of the royal palace with a loud SPLASH!

The king and his counselor, a wise man indeed, happened to be standing nearby, discussing the king's proposed birthday speech. Both had their beautiful robes splashed with water. They looked into the pond and saw the tortoise swimming towards them.

"Poor tortoise," cried the king, "are you hurt? Did you crack your shell? Where did you come from? How did you drop from the sky? Can a tortoise fly? Are you a special tortoise? Perhaps you know magic. Or did someone toss you over the wall and into my pond? Tell me who the scoundrel is and I'll deal with him harshly. Or are you an angel sent from the heavens to give me a message? Yes, that's it, a birthday message from the gods. Oh joy, and what is the message? Wait, don't tell me. I am unworthy. There is no message for me. But if I am unworthy, then why are you here? Go ahead and tell me. Yes, tell me everything. I'll include your wonderful message in my speech. I know my subjects will want to hear every word."

The tortoise said nothing and slowly swam to the edge of the pond.

The wise counselor had seen everything and decided that the moment had arrived to give the king some advice.

"Oh Mighty, Powerful, and Wise Ruler," he said. "Two geese carried the tortoise in flight by holding a stick in their beaks. By biting into the stick, the tortoise was able to fly with them. Some children laughed at the tortoise and she grew angry. Then she made a large mistake by snapping back at them. Thus she fell out of the sky and into your pond. This is what befalls those who cannot hold their tongues."

The king understood the counselor's warning. He decided then and there to do more listening than talking. He canceled his five-hour birthday speech and instead gave a party for Mistress Tortoise, who lived happily in the courtyard pond for the rest of her long life.

Leopard's Magnificent Drum

Africa (Ghana)

Leopard owned the most magnificent drum in all of Africa. It stood as tall as a zebra. It was painted with rainbow colors. Its sides were covered with skilled carvings. Thin and strong cowhide stretched across its top, creating a deep, rich, and resonant sound. Leopard was proud of his drum and never allowed anyone else to play it. The jungle animals knew that Leopard was as fierce as the drum was fine and left him alone with his treasure.

One day the God of the Sky called all the animals, except for Leopard, to his kingdom in the clouds. He announced that he was planning a special ceremony for the following week. Sky

God's ceremonies were spectacular events, and everyone wanted to attend.

"The ceremony will be held in seven days," said Sky God. "To make it special, I wish to borrow Leopard's drum and have it played for the dancing. If one of you is brave enough to bring me the drum, I'll honor you with one wish granted."

"I'll get the drum for you," trumpeted Elephant. "I'm as brave as I am big!"

Elephant returned to the jungle and spoke with Leopard. "Sky God wishes to borrow your drum for his party. I'm here to get it for him."

Leopard curled his long tail around his beautiful instrument and snarled, "Get away from my drum or die, you overgrown anteater."

Elephant turned and ran back to Sky God, muttering, "Leopard said no."

"I'll get it for you," grunted Gorilla. "Leopard doesn't frighten me."

Gorilla climbed back down to the jungle and approached Leopard. "Let me take your drum, and I won't break you in half," said Gorilla.

"Leave me alone, and I won't rip open your stomach," growled Leopard.

Gorilla ran back to Sky God and said, "Leopard said no."

"Let me do it," said Vulture. "I always clean up everyone's messes."

Vulture flew down to Leopard and squawked, "Let me take the drum now, and I won't pick your bones clean later."

"I'll pick *your* bones out of my teeth if you don't fly away," snapped Leopard.

Vulture flapped her large wings and returned to Sky God. "Leopard says no," she said with a disappointed sigh.

Many other animals tried to get the drum for the celebration. Lion tried. Rhinoceros tried. Zebra tried. Monkey tried. Jackal tried. They all failed.

Finally, Turtle, who at that time had a soft back and slow crawl, said, "I will bring you the drum, Oh Mighty God of the Sky."

The other animals laughed and Crocodile said, "You are too small and too weak. Leopard will eat you whole."

"Quiet!" demanded Sky God. "Everyone who has tried has failed. Turtle can do no worse."

Turtle crawled down to Leopard's den. "Have you come for my drum, like all the others?" he asked.

"Oh no," said Turtle. "I'm here to examine your inferior drum. Sky God has made a new and wondrous drum for himself, and he wants to know all the ways in which it is superior to yours."

"There is no drum better than mine. Mine is the finest there is," said Leopard.

"Actually," explained Turtle, "your drum

looks a bit small in comparison to Sky God's. I mean, Sky God can climb inside his drum and no one can see him."

"Are you saying I can't do the same? My drum is big enough to hold me."

"I respectfully doubt that, Leopard," said Turtle. "Your drum could never hold all of you. What about your long tail? Wouldn't it hang out?"

"Just watch," said Leopard. He laid his wonderful drum on its side and crawled inside through its open bottom. It was an extremely tight fit, and he had to squeeze his hindquarters together to get himself completely in.

"Just as I thought," said Turtle. "Your tail hangs out. I'll go now and tell Sky God how much larger his drum is."

Leopard squeezed and pulled his long tail inside until only the tip was showing.

"Too bad," said Turtle. "You almost had it, but not quite. I'll tell Sky God ..."

Leopard grunted and pulled and wriggled until the tip of his tail was inside the cramped space. Turtle heard a muffled voice say, "I'm in, I'm in."

"Yes, you are," said Turtle, and he quickly covered over the end of the drum with a strong piece of cowhide and fastened it with a strong vine. Leopard was trapped. Turtle began to drag it back to Sky God's house. It was slow going. Each time he stopped to rest, he pounded on the drum to signal his success.

When he finally arrived, the other animals looked upon Turtle with jealous eyes. They were very angry because he had succeeded where they had failed.

Turtle spoke to Sky God, "Here is Leopard's drum as I promised. Inside the drum is Leopard himself. He is angry and has complained all the way."

Sky God was pleased with Turtle and asked,

"What shall I do with the selfish Leopard? Shall I kill him?"

"No, please don't kill me," said a small voice from inside the drum. "I'm sorry that I was so selfish. You can have my drum for your ceremony and any other time you want it, great God of the Sky."

"Leopard has spoken," said Sky God. "Let him go free."

Turtle removed the cowhide from the drum's bottom and Leopard backed out of the confined space, tail first. Because he couldn't see where he was going, he backed right into Sky God's cooking fire. His tail and body were burned in several places by the glowing hot embers. Leopard leaped into the air with a loud "YELP!" and ran back down to the jungle. The burned patches on his brown hide remained and that is why all leopards have dark spots today.

Sky God then said to Turtle, "You will be

my special guest and play the drum at the ceremony. You have also earned one wish fulfilled.
What will it be?"

Turtle looked at all the other animals who
were still angry with him and said, "Give me a
hard shell to wear on my back. I will need the
protection."

Sky God made it so, and that is why Turtle
carries his hard shell wherever he goes, even to
this day.

The Dancing Turtle

South America
(from the Indigenous Peoples of Brazil)

Long ago, on the bank of the mighty Amazon River, Turtle played her flute while enjoying the sun. She played the high notes and the low notes. She played the fast ones and the slow ones. She played her flute with such skill and joy that before long she felt like dancing! Turtle laid her flute down and began to dance her happiest dance. Around and around she twirled, going this way and that. She bobbed and weaved and jumped and crawled, dancing all the while. Then she stopped. Her dance was done. She pulled her head and legs into her shell and went to sleep.

Being asleep, she didn't notice the two dark eyes of a man peering at her from behind a broad, green leaf. She didn't hear the rumble of hunger in his stomach. And she didn't feel his strong brown hand grab hold of her shell until it was too late.

"Got you!" he cried. "My family will soon feast on turtle soup."

He shoved Turtle and her flute into the bag he carried over his shoulder and began the long walk to his home. It was dark by the time he arrived.

He took Turtle and her flute from his bag and said to his three children, "Look at the fat turtle I've caught. I heard a flute playing in the forest and followed the sweet sounds to the edge of the river. There I saw Turtle dancing, and when she finished, she went to sleep. It was easy to catch her. I'll put her in the cage, and we will make a fine soup with her tomorrow."

The man put Turtle in a cage made of strong sticks. He tied the small door shut with a long leather thong. Turtle couldn't escape, and she spent a fearful night in captivity.

In the morning the father decided to work in the fields. He told his children, "Stay home and take care of the turtle. Don't let her out of the cage for any reason. I'll be home when the sun goes down and we'll cook her for supper."

The man picked up his hoe and walked to the fields. The children played games near the hut and ran over to peek into Turtle's cage every chance they got. Turtle sat and thought and thought about her predicament. Then she had an idea. She picked up her flute and began to play. She played the high notes and the low ones. She played the fast ones and the slow ones. She played so sweetly and so well that the children ran to the cage, and said, "Play more,

Turtle. Please play more!"

"I can do more than play tunes," answered Turtle. "I can dance as well."

The children had never seen a turtle dance before and said, "You can't dance. Turtles can't dance. You're trying to trick us."

"I couldn't trick you," said Turtle. "Children are too smart. All the forest animals know better than to try to trick children."

"Would you try to escape if we let you out?" asked one of the children.

"Of course not," said Turtle. "I only want to show you how well I can dance. But if you don't want to see me dance, then I'll put my flute away and go back to sleep."

"No!" cried the children. "You must show us." They untied the long leather thong, opened the small door, and took Turtle out of the cage. Turtle played her flute. She played the high notes and the low notes. She played the fast ones and the slow ones. She played her flute with such skill and joy that she felt like dancing! Turtle laid down her flute and began to dance her happiest dance. Around and around she twirled, going this way and that. She bobbed and weaved and jumped and crawled, dancing all the while. Then she stopped. Her dance was done.

"Again!" cried the children, "Dance again!"

"Yes," said Turtle, "just as soon as I catch my breath. Please carry me over to the shade trees, where I can cool down."

The children picked her up and carried her to the edge of the forest where the largest of the shade trees stood. "I'll take a little nap," said Turtle, "and then I'll be ready to dance again. Go and play your games. I'll play my flute when I've rested."

The children left and Turtle began crawling through the jungle undergrowth. She didn't rest or play her flute until she was safely home by the river. When the children grew tired of their games, they ran back to the shade trees, calling, "Turtle, where are you, Turtle? You said you would dance for us again. Where are you hiding?"

There was no answer. They realized that Turtle had tricked them after all. They also realized that their father would be angry.

They sat on the ground and thought and thought. Soon they had an idea. They searched for and found a large rock shaped like Turtle's shell. They painted the rock so that it looked just like Turtle and placed it in the cage. They secured the small door with the long leather thong and hoped for the best.

Their hungry father arrived home as the sunlight was fading. He put a pot of water on the fire and waited for it to boil. Then he opened the cage and pulled Turtle from inside. "She's still asleep," he whispered to his children, "and she's weighs more than I remembered."

He plopped the painted stone into the pot and said, "Bring the big serving platter, the one made of hardened clay. It will soon be time to eat."

The children were frightened, but said nothing. They brought the platter and set it before their father. He took the rock from the pot and dropped it onto the plate. The plate broke into many pieces. The father looked carefully at the rock. Then he looked even more carefully at his children.

"You let Turtle out of her cage, didn't you?"

"Yes, Father, we're sorry," said the children. "Turtle said she wouldn't trick us and then she did."

"Turtle is very clever," he said, "more clever than I thought. Don't worry, children. I'll try to catch her again tomorrow, and then we'll have our turtle soup."

Did he ever catch Turtle again? What do you think?

Wayamba the Turtle

Australia (Aboriginal)

Long ago a man called Wayamba fell in love with a lizard called Oolah. She belonged to the lizard tribe, and Wayamba belonged to the human tribe. Oolah said she wouldn't marry outside her tribe. Wayamba decided that he couldn't live without her. He made a plan to steal her.

One day Oolah and her three children were alone on the Mirria flat digging for yams. Wayamba hid behind a large Mirria bush, and when one of the children wandered near, he leaped out and grabbed him. Hearing her child's cry, Oolah dropped her digging stick and ran to him.

Wayamba stepped forward. He looked fierce in his warrior's paint and carried many weapons. "You must go with me to the human camp, Oolah," he said to the frightened lizard. "You will be my wife, and I will take care of you and your children."

"Never!" cried Oolah. "My tribe will not allow you to steal me. Let me and my children go."

Wayamba wouldn't listen and took the lizard family to the human camp. The humans asked Wayamba if Oolah had come willingly.

"No," said Wayamba. "I had to force her. I must have her. I will not give her back."

"That is a bad thing," they said. "Oolah's tribe will come after her and the children. They will fight for her. We will not help you. We will not fight for you. *You* must be responsible for your actions."

Soon thereafter, Oolah's tribe crossed the

wide plain and came to the human camp. They had come to fight. Their faces and bodies wore the paint of battle, and they carried many long spears and deadly boomerangs.

The human chief spoke to the angry lizards and said, "Wayamba was wrong to steal your daughter. We will not defend him. Your fight is with him alone."

Wayamba spoke to the lizards. "I am not afraid of you. I will fight all of you on the Mirria flat." He ran to his hut and selected his two largest wooden shields, called boreens. He tied one to the front of his body and tied the other to his back. He grabbed his spear and boomerang and ran out of the village and onto the plain. When he reached the center of the flat, Wayamba turned to face the lizards who were running close behind.

The battle began when Wayamba yelled, "Come on, let's see what you can do!"

The lizard warriors threw their spears just as Wayamba pulled his arms and ducked his head inside his shields. He wasn't hurt, and again he yelled, "Come on, you will have to do better than that!"

Boomerangs whizzed through the air, and again Wayamba pulled his arms and head inside. He escaped from harm a second time.

Suddenly the lizards rushed toward him, and Wayamba was forced to run for his life. He dropped his weapons and fled to a small, nearby river. The lizards were close behind as he waded and splashed into the water. Then he dove to the sandy bottom. The warriors gathered at river's edge and held their spears high, waiting for him to surface. They waited and waited, but Wayamba never came up for air.

Many days later, a new creature was spotted swimming in the river. It had a strong, round shell on it's back. They caught it and it pulled its head and legs inside.

"It's Wayamba," they said.

And this is how the turtle that swims in the creeks and small rivers came to be.

The Monkey's Liver

Japan

D ragon King and Queen lived in the Emerald Palace at the bottom of the sea. One day Dragon Queen fell ill. The Royal Physician, an octopus named Dr. Arms, said that to get well the queen had to eat the liver of a monkey.

"Summon faithful Sea Turtle," said Dragon King. "He will swim to the surface and bring Monkey to us."

Turtle swam up, up, and up until he reached the ocean's surface, and then he swam to the nearest jungle island. He crawled slowly up the sandy shore and came to a large grove of coconut trees. Inquisitive Monkey peered down from the top of the highest tree and asked, "Why have you come to visit me, Great Green Turtle from the sea?"

"Friend Monkey," replied Turtle, "Dragon King wishes to invite you to a royal feast. Hop onto my back, and I'll carry you to the Emerald Palace."

Monkey was delighted! He scurried down from the coconuts, leaped upon Turtle's shell, and held on tight.

Turtle crawled back into the sea and swam down, down, and down, all the way to the dragon's lair. When they arrived at the outer gate, Turtle said to Monkey, "Hop off and wait. I must tell the King and Queen of your arrival."

Turtle swam away, leaving Monkey with Captain Jellyfish, the Royal Guardian of the Gate. Captain Jellyfish stood stiffly at attention, paying little heed to Monkey. Monkey puffed up his small chest and said, "I've been invited to dine with Dragon King and Queen."

"You wouldn't be so proud if you knew why they've invited you," said Captain Jellyfish.

"Isn't it because they want my company?" asked Monkey.

"It's because of your liver. Dragon Queen wants to eat your liver," replied Captain Jellyfish.

Realizing that he was in real trouble, Monkey made a plan.

When Turtle returned to take him inside, he said, "I'm so very sorry to trouble you, Sea Turtle, but could we make a quick trip back to my island before the feast begins? I've done something quite silly. I've left my liver up in the coconut tree. I forgot it in all the excitement about coming, and now I fear that Talking Parrot will steal it."

"Oh dear," said Turtle, "this is serious! Quick, climb onto my back. We must go get it!"

Up, up, and up they swam, right back to the

island. Monkey leaped from Turtle's shell onto the sand and scampered to the top of the coconut tree.

"Please hurry," hollered Turtle. "Dragon King and Queen are growing impatient."

Monkey tossed a ripe coconut down to Turtle and it bounced off his hard shell and rolled onto the sand. "Take the coconut to them and tell them to start without me," he said. "I've decided to stay home and keep my liver for myself!"

Turtle swam back home and told Dragon King what happened. "It must have been Captain Jellyfish who told Monkey what we were after," explained Turtle.

"Captain Jellyfish must be punished," declared Dragon King. "From this day forward, he will no longer be Royal Guardian of the Gate. Nor will he have bones with which to stand erect. Let him float about the oceans wide, following the currents wherever they carry him."

That is why today jellyfish have no bones. And that is also why monkeys are never seen riding on the back of sea turtles.

Tortoise and the Sweet Potatoes

South Africa

H are was a trickster, a rascal, and a cheat. He was too clever for his own good, and his own good was what his cleverness usually rewarded ... except when he met up with Tortoise.

Tortoise was a helper, a giver, and a friend. She was as wise as she was clever, and her wisdom helped her out of many tight spots, especially when Hare was involved.

This is the story of what happened one day when the mischievous Hare decided to trick the thoughtful Tortoise.

Hare hopped up to Tortoise's pond and said, "I have an idea that will help both of us. Let's get some hoes and till a field. We can plant seeds and grow sweet potatoes. We'll divide the crop after the harvest, half for you and half for me."

Tortoise loved the taste of sweet potatoes and liked the idea of sharing the hard work involved in growing them. "I'll agree," she said, "if after the harvest and division, I get to choose my half of the potatoes. And if you try to cheat me out of my share, I get them all, yours and mine."

"I would *never* try to cheat someone as smart as you, Miss Tortoise," said Hare, and he hopped off to get the hoes.

They worked hard together, tilling the land and planting the seed. Then, with the help of nature's sun, wind, and rain, the sweet potatoes began to grow beneath the earth. Both Hare and Tortoise checked on their field each day, and whenever a weed was spotted, it was quickly removed. After several months, it was time to harvest the crop.

Tortoise watched every move made by Hare so that she wasn't cheated. She used her strong short legs and powerful claws to loosen the dirt while Hare used his digging stick to pry the potatoes out of the ground. After working in the hot sun for most of the day, they had accumulated a large pile of delicious sweet potatoes.

"I'll divide them into two groups, Miss Tortoise, and you can choose the one you want," said Hare.

"That was our agreement, Mr. Hare, and I'm pleased that I didn't have to remind you," she said aloud. But she was thinking, *Now is the time I'll have to be careful. He is such a sneak!*

After the crop was divided into two equal piles, Tortoise chose the one closest to her. "I like the looks of it," she explained. She filled a gunny sack with her share, just as Hare filled a sack with his pile.

When both sacks were completely full, Hare said, "Quiet, I think I hear something. It may be the Wild Boar family. You know how much they like sweet potatoes. If they find us, we'll lose all. Quickly, hide your sack in the bushes and I'll hide mine. Then we can scout around the outside of the field to make sure that the Boars haven't discovered us."

So this is his game, is it? Tortoise asked herself. She pushed her heavy sack into the forest and hid it in the roots of a baobab tree. Then she quickly crawled back to the field in time to see Hare hide his share beneath the nearby bushes. Realizing that Hare would try to find and steal her sack as soon as she went in search of the Boar Family, Tortoise waited until Hare hopped away, and then stole *his* sack. She carried it on her back and hid it in the nearby bushes, just as Hare told her to do with her own. Then she untied Hare's sack, crawled inside burrowing deep into the sweet potatoes, and waited.

Hare soon came by, saw his own sack, and said, "And what do we have sitting here? It looks like Miss Tortoise's sack just waiting for me. And look at how careless she is. The top is open. I'll have to tie it up tight and take it home. When I sneak back tonight and get my own bag, I'll have the entire crop, just as I planned."

Tortoise heard every word and started chuckling to herself, "This is going to be a heavy load for Hare to carry all by himself. I'd better help him out." Thus she began to eat the ripe sweet potatoes in the sack, one by one as Hare dragged the sack home. It was a good thing she was hungry, since there were so many to devour. It took her as long to finish the sackful as it took Hare to lug it home.

Once there, he opened the sack, saying, "I'll just eat a few before I hop back to get my sack." He reached in and felt around in the emptiness until he found Tortoise's hard shell. "Oh, here is a big one. I'll eat it and then I'll be full."

He pulled Miss Tortoise out and was so surprised to see her that he dropped her on the ground. He looked into the empty sack, then at her, and cried, "Miss Tortoise! What are you doing here? And where are your sweet potatoes?"

"My sweet potatoes are safe, just don't you worry Mr. Hare. The potatoes which you carried home and I so enjoyed were your very own. And that's just what you deserve for trying to cheat me."

Hare was very angry and said, "You'll never beat me back to the field, and when I get there, I'll take the other sack."

"Let the race begin," said Tortoise as she began crawling. Hare bounded into the air and was gone in a flash. He arrived at the field long before Tortoise and began looking under every bush, but he couldn't find the second sack. He looked and looked. Then he sat down and cried. Miss Tortoise was simply too clever for him, and he swore that he would never try to cheat her again.

Meanwhile, Tortoise kept crawling toward the baobab tree, knowing that the second sack of sweet potatoes would be even more delicious than the first.

Father Wind and His Four Sons

Native American
(from the Yuchi People of the Southeast)

Father Wind lived in the sky with his four sons. One day the oldest son said, "Father, I have always been curious about the earth. I want to explore the land and sea and learn all that I can."

"Yes," agreed Father Wind, "that is an excellent plan. Take your brother, my second born, with you. It is difficult to travel alone."

The two brothers flew down to the earth and began their explorations. They were gone a long, long time. Father Wind grew worried and asked his two youngest sons to travel to the earth.

"Find your older brothers and bring them

back to me," he said.

They left the next morning and they also were gone for a long, long time. Father Wind grew even more worried and spoke to his friend and advisor, Old Turtle. "Why haven't my sons returned home?" he asked.

"I do not know," said Old Turtle. "Just as there is beauty upon the earth, so there is danger. Now is the time to follow after your children and bring them home. I will travel with you. Bring your pipe, the one with the magic smoke."

Father Wind rode upon Old Turtle's strong back all the way down to the earth. They arrived in the West and searched for many days and nights. Father Wind blew and blew, calling out for his four lost sons. Father Wind blew so hard that trees bent over and the animals and birds feared for their lives. Still, the boys did not answer.

One day Old Turtle and Father Wind came

to a deep lake. "I have a bad feeling," said Old Turtle. "Something is wrong with this place. Your sons are near, yet they are not here."

They saw a large, dark cave on the other side of the lake. Smoke was coming from inside.

"We'll visit the cave-dweller," said Old Turtle. Father Wind sat on his back, and they swam to the far shore. An ugly, old crone, a witch of a woman with bent back and bad breath, emerged from the cave.

"Beware," Old Turtle whispered to Father Wind. "She is filled with evil."

The woman smiled with a crooked grin and said, "You are welcome here. I always like to visit with strangers for they have such interesting stories to tell. Come into my cave and smoke the pipe of peace with me."

"Thank you," said Father Wind. "I have my pipe right here."

"Put it away, put it away," she said. "My pipe is

already packed with a very special tobacco leaf."

"No," said Father Wind. "We will smoke my pipe."

"Never!" cried the crone. "We will smoke mine!"

So saying, she lit her pipe and puffed hard. A foul-smelling smoke filled the cave.

"It's poison," said Old Turtle. "Light your pipe. Battle her with your magic smoke!"

Father Wind lit his long pipe and puffed and puffed. His smoke intermingled with hers and began to overtake it. The old woman puffed faster and faster, but she didn't stand a chance against the powerful lungs of Father Wind. His magic smoke encircled her and slowly choked the life out of her. When she was dead, the evil pipe fell out of her hands and broke in half on the stone floor.

Old Turtle and Father Wind walked outside the cave and heard four ghostly voices calling:

"Here, Father. Here we are. In the tree. Get

us out. Hurry, Father."

The voices came from inside a towering tree standing beside the lake. The tree was dead.

"Your sons are gone," said Old Turtle. "They were killed by the old woman and put in this tree. It is the voice of their spirits that call to you."

Four tears rolled down the cheeks of Father Wind. "What can I do to bring them back?" he asked.

"Cut the tree down and let it fall into the lake. Then use your breath," explained Old Turtle. Using a sharp axe, Father Wind chopped down the dead tree. It fell into the water with a loud splash. Then he kneeled on the ground and began to breathe into the water. He blew, and blew, and blew so hard that the lake churned and foamed. Waves rose higher than the surrounding trees, and several fish were left flopping on the ground. Finally, Father Wind was out of breath, and the lake grew calm again. Then something wonderful happened. One by one, the four boys rose up out of the water and stood before their father.

The oldest son said, "You have breathed the gift of life into us, Father. We thank you."

The second son said, "The old woman tricked us into smoking her killing-weed. Then she put us into this tree."

The third son said, "We can't go home with you, Father. Since we were reborn on the earth, it is upon the earth we must forever stay."

The youngest son said, "Do not cry for us, Father. We will be the earth winds. Your oldest son will be the cold North Wind. Your second born will be the warm West Wind. Your third son will be the strong East Wind. And I, your youngest, will be the gentle South Wind. We will love the earth and help bring the four seasons."

Old Turtle spoke. "This is a wise plan. It

will help the earth."

"Then let it be so," said Father Wind, and he and Old Turtle said farewell and went on their way home.

And ever since that long-ago time, Father Wind has ridden down to earth on Old Turtle's strong back to visit with his four sons. He is always so happy to see them that he blows too hard, and then trees and even houses fall to the ground. But Father Wind never stays too long. Like his sons, he loves the earth, and doesn't want to hurt her. That is what the old Yuchi say.

The Banana Bet

Central America (Panama)

One day old Mama Tortoise decided to have a party for her many children. Thinking that two large bunches of ripe bananas would be enough to feed them, she set out for the grove. Mama Tortoise crawled up to the foot of the tallest tree, the one with the largest and ripest bananas hanging in bunches, and sighed.

There they are, she said to herself, *the perfect bananas. But how will I get them down to the ground?* She thought and thought and suddenly had an idea. *I'll get that old monkey to help. He's always trying to get the best of me. Perhaps I'll trick him.*

It wasn't long before Mr. Monkey showed

up. He had been down at the seashore catching crabs with his fast hands. Now he was heading home for a nap.

"Hello, Mr. Monkey," said Mama Tortoise. "Are you feeling strong today?"

"I always feel strong," replied the monkey. "Why do you ask?"

"It's just that I've been climbing up trees for several weeks, and I'm getting to be quite fast. In fact, I would like to race you to the top of this tall banana tree."

Mr. Monkey laughed and laughed. "You, a crawling tortoise, beat me, a climbing monkey, to the top of a tree? That's impossible! It simply couldn't happen. You would lose every time."

"I'll bet you two bunches of bananas that I can beat you," she said.

"Done," said Mr. Monkey. "But when you lose, remember that you offered the bet, not I."

Parrot agreed to start and judge the race.

"Uno, dos, tres ... begin climbing!" she squawked.

Mr. Monkey gripped the tree with his strong hands and nimble feet and rushed to the top as fast as a toucan in flight. Then he sat on the highest branch to catch his breath and watched Mama Tortoise begin her long and difficult climb. She was so slow that the monkey stretched out on the branch and took a nap.

When Mama Tortoise finally arrived at the top, huffing and puffing, Parrot screeched, "Monkey wins, Monkey wins!"

Mr. Monkey laughed and laughed and swung from branch to branch to celebrate his victory.

"You have won fairly," gasped Mama Tortoise. "I owe you two large bunches of bananas. I wonder, however, if you would be interested in a second wager. This time, I'll bet you four ripe bunches that I can beat you to the ground."

"Never!" screeched Mr. Monkey, "Never! Never! You couldn't beat me if I had my hands tied behind my back and I scooted down this tree using only my legs. I'm ten times faster than you. I'm a hundred times faster!"

"Are you going to keep on bragging, or do you agree to the bet?" asked Mama Tortoise.

"You're on," said the monkey.

Again Parrot agreed to referee. "Uno, dos, tres ... begin!" she squawked.

Mama Tortoise then did something quite surprising. She pulled her head and feet and tail into her hard shell and dropped from the branch like a rock. She fell straight down to the soft ground in a flash and landed safely in the soft sand.

Mr. Monkey blinked several times and couldn't believe what he had just witnessed. He was just beginning his rapid descent, and there she was, already on the ground. When he finally reached the bottom of the tree, Parrot squawked, "Tortoise wins, Tortoise wins!"

Mrs. Tortoise grinned and said, "Let's figure out the results, Mr. Monkey. I've won four bunches of bananas from you, and you've won two from me. That means that you only have to pay me two bunches, and we'll be even. Would you be kind enough to get them for me now? I have a party to give."

Mr. Monkey paid his debt, but he wasn't happy. He didn't think that it was right that Mama Tortoise was more clever than he.

The Hot Water Test

Africa (Nigeria)

I japa,* which is the Nigerian name for tortoise, was sometimes lazy, and he hadn't worked in his growing field for several months. His storehouse was empty, and his family complained of hunger.

It was the season of yams. The chief's servants told the animals to come to the royal field to harvest the yams. Everyone had to help, and the chief would keep all the yams for himself. Ijapa felt that this was unfair and devised a clever plan.

That night he sneaked into the chief's field and dug a small but deep hole in the ground.

∘ Ijapa is pronounced Ee-jah-pah

Using branches and long grass, he was able to camouflage the top of the hole. Satisfied with his work, he went on home.

Ijapa returned the following morning, along with all the other animals, and reported for work. Each animal was given a basket and a digging stick and told to go to work. Ijapa was very slow to fill his basket. Each time he put a yam inside he dropped the next one down his secret hole. A yam for the basket and a yam for the hole ... a yam for the basket and a yam for the hole ... all day long. The harvest was complete with the setting of the sun. The chief's storehouse was full, and all the tired animals went home to their families.

Ijapa waited until the moon was high before he returned to the chief's field. He carried his own basket and filled it up with the stolen yams. He made several trips from the secret hole to his farm and back, and by sunrise his storehouse was full. Ijapa was pleased with his night's work and boasted to his wife, "They will never figure it out. I'm too clever for the lot of them."

But they did figure it out. The other animals found the empty hole and saw the path through the long grass that lead straight to Ijapa's farm. They opened the door to his storehouse and found the yams. The animals were angry and told the chief that Ijapa was a thief. The chief summoned Ijapa and told him that he would have to stand trial.

"I ask you directly, Ijapa," said the chief, "did you steal my yams?"

"Oh no, never, wise chief! I'm completely innocent. I would never steal from you," answered Ijapa.

"The other animals say that there is a path from my field to your storehouse which is now full. How do you explain that?"

"What path?" asked Ijapa. "Oh, you must

mean the path I made when I came to work for you and then followed home again."

"I think you are lying to me, Ijapa. The other animals have made a good case against you. But I want to be fair in my judgment. I will find you guilty as charged, or you can take the hot water test to prove your innocence."

"I'll take the hot water test," gulped the tortoise.

The chief's servants lit a fire under a large pot of water. When the water was boiling hot, the chief addressed the crowd of animals who had come to witness the trial. "Ijapa must drink a gourd full of hot water. If he is innocent as he claims, he will not be burned. If he is guilty, however, he will suffer greatly."

Ijapa then spoke. "Oh Great Chief, I will be found innocent. This I already know. I'll be set free and still you will not know who the real thief is. Any of the animals who worked in your field yesterday could be guilty. We should all be tested. Only then will you know for certain."

"No!" yelled Deer. "I don't want to be tested."

"Nor I!" said Monkey. "It isn't fair!"

"We didn't steal from you," said Rabbit. "It was Ijapa."

"How am I to know that?" asked the chief. "Ijapa has made a good point. If you don't want to take the test, then you must have something to hide. Everyone will drink from the cup of truth."

"Since I'm first accused, let me be the last to drink," said the tortoise.

"Agreed," said the chief. "And you shall serve the water to the others."

Ijapa filled a gourd with the boiling water and gave it to Goat. Goat drank it down and it burned his mouth. The pain was great and he bleated pitifully. Ijapa filled the gourd for the python and she drank. The water burned all the long way down to her stomach, and she cried and cried. Ijapa filled the gourd for lion, and he too roared in pain. Ijapa filled the gourd for everyone, and everyone suffered.

Then it was Ijapa's turn to take the test. He filled the gourd again and held it above his head for all to see. Then he spoke to the crowd.

"I, Ijapa, friend to all and loyal to our chief, have been unfairly accused of a crime I didn't commit. Now I will drink this boiling water to prove my innocence. Before I take the first sip, however, I want all of you to see that I didn't cheat when I filled the gourd. It isn't half full, nor is it three-quarters full. It's filled to the very top. Look, Oh Wise Chief, see that it is full to the top."

The chief looked and said, "Yes, Ijapa, it is full to the top."

The tortoise said, "Look, all you servants of the chief, it is full to the top."

The servants looked and cried, "Yes, Ijapa, we see that it is full to the top."

"Look, all the deer family, it is full to the top."

The deer looked and called back, "Yes, Ijapa, we see it. It is full to the top."

"Look, all you monkeys, it is full to the top."

The monkeys looked and said, "Yes, Ijapa, your gourd is full to the top."

"Look, all you rabbits, I didn't cheat. My gourd is full to the top."

The rabbits looked and said, "Yes, Ijapa, your gourd is full to the top."

And so it went. Ijapa called out to each of the animal families present to witness his full gourd, and each responded accordingly. Of course, the boiling water had time to cool down during all the witnessing, and this is just what Ijapa had in mind.

When he finally drank his gourd full of warm water, he didn't cry out or even shed a single tear. The chief was satisfied that Ijapa was innocent.

The other animals were blamed for the theft and had to give the chief all the yams they had grown in their own gardens. They stayed angry with Ijapa for a very long time.

And ever since, whenever someone falsely accuses another, the people say, "When Ijapa blames someone else, he must have something to hide."

Notes

Motifs given are from Margaret Read MacDonald, *The Storyteller's Sourcebook: A Subject, Title, and Motif Index to Folklore Collections for Children*. (Detroit: Gale/Neal-Schuman, 1982).

Why California Has Earthquakes
Native American (Gabrielino People of California), page 15

Motif A815, *Earth erected on the back of a Turtle floating in primeval water.*

This is an authentic Native American myth initially collected by anthropologist, Dr. C. Hart Merriam. He related it to Anne B. Fisher, and I discovered it in her collection. The Gabrielino Natives lived around the Channel Islands and from Santa Barbara south to Los Angeles. Use a map to show the shape of California when sharing it with younger listeners.

See *Stories California Indians Told* by Anne B. Fisher (Berkeley, CA: Parnassus Press, 1957) pp. 10-15.

The Courting of Miss Python

Central Africa (Congo), page 23

Motif F914.0.1, *Tortoise claims to like all of Rock Python's attentions—embrace, toss in air, swallowing, etc. Rock Python regurgitates him and allows to wed daughter.*

I emphasize Turtle's innate confidence and impeccable manners over his cleverness when telling this tale. It provides him with a depth of character not often found in folktales.

For another version, see *The Magic Drum: Tales From Central Africa* by W.F.P. Burton (NY: Criterion Books, 1961) pp. 98-101.

The Talkative King

India, page 31

Motif J2357, *Tortoise speaks and loses his hold on the stick. He is being carried through the air by a bird.*

In this tale, also known as "The Tortoise and the Geese," I enjoy gently shifting the emphasis from the tortoise to the talkative king. The value of the "lesson" is heightened. A good choice for business executives as well as noisy classrooms.

For another version, see *Twenty Jataka Tales* by Noor Inayat (Philadelphia: David McKay Co., 1939) pp. 39-41.

Leopard's Magnificent Drum

Africa (Ghana), page 37

Motif K714.2.5, *Turtle tells Osebo (leopard) that his drum is smaller than Nyame's (Sky-God) because Osebo can get into Nyame's drum. Osebo enters drum and is trapped.*

In addition to explaining why the turtle has a hard shell and why the leopard has spots, this tale celebrates Turtle's confidence and his cleverness. In this adventure, Turtle's resourcefulness rivals that of the famous African Trickster, Anansi.

For another version, see *The Hat Shaking Dance and Other Ashanti Tales from Ghana* by Harold Courlander (NY: Harcourt, Brace & World, 1957) pp. 32-7.

The Dancing Turtle

South America (Indigenous People of Brazil), page 47

Motif K571.0.2, *Turtle playing flute and dancing untied by children.*

Initially collected by José Vieira Coutode Magalhães in *O selvagem,* Rio de Janeiro, 1876, this is another story in which Turtle uses her wit to survive. More than one of my younger listeners over the years has expressed surprise that Turtle would actually lie to children.

For another version, see *The King of the Mountains: A Treasury of Latin American Folk Stories* by M.A. Jagendorf and R.S. Boggs (NY: Vanguard Press, 1960) pp. 55-9.

Wayamba the Turtle

Australia (Aboriginal), page 57

Motif A2312.1.0.3, *Lizard hides from enemies behind shields and dives into creek. Turns into turtle.*

The Indigenous peoples of Australia may be a race older than the Egyptians. My favorite turtle creation myth, "Wayamba" reveals much about aboriginal justice.

The motif describes Wayamba as a Lizard prior to transformation into a turtle. My research suggests otherwise. Wayamba is described as "the little black fellow" in one of the earliest versions (cited below). It is also the story from which all other written versions seem to originate.

See *Folktales of All Nations* by F.L. Lee (NY: Tudor Publishing Co., 1930 & 1946) pp. 156-7.

The Monkey's Liver

Japan, page 63

Motif K544.1, *Jellyfish sent to fetch monkey to Dragon Queen's palace. Jellyfish tells Monkey Queen plans to eat his liver and Monkey claims he left it at home. Jellyfish is beaten to a pulp for failure.*

There are many variants of this popular Japanese tale, and the one I use here, in which Sea Turtle is messenger and Jellyfish, gatekeeper, can also be found in the collection cited below. In yet another variant, it's Monkey's heart rather than his liver that is desired by Dragon Queen. Create fun voices for Dragon King, Monkey, Turtle, and especially Captain Jellyfish.

For a similar variant, see *Magic Animals of Japan* by Davis Pratt and Elsa Kula (Berkeley: Parnassus Press, 1967) pp. 10-11.

Tortoise and the Sweet Potatoes
South Africa, page 69

Motif K335.0.1.2, *Hare tricks tortoise but she crawls into bag and eats as he runs.*

It's a delight to show Turtle outwitting other famous Tricksters. This tale is based on a story in Henri Junod's The Life of a South African Tribe, Vol. 2, (London: Macmillan & Co., 1927).

I initially discovered it in the collection entitled *The Ox of the Wonderful Horns and Other African Folktales* by Ashley Bryan (NY: Antheneum, 1971) pp. 22-8.

Father Wind and His Four Sons
Native American (Yuchi People of the Southeast), page 77

Motif A1120, *Establishment of present order: winds.*

I appreciate Turtle's secondary roles as trusted advisor as well as transporter in this tale of the origin of the four winds. The powerful image of Father Wind riding down to earth on Turtle's back is one to savor in the telling.

For another version, see *Native American Legends* by George E. Lankford (Little Rock: August House, 1987) pp. 70-72.

The Banana Bet

Central America (Panama), page 85

Motif K15.2 *Climbing match. Monkey reaches top of tree first. Turtle bets double he can reach ground first. Jumps.*

Mama Tortoise's winning strategy usually comes as a surprise to listeners. Her descent from tree to ground should occur with swift and sure verbal strokes. Then watch the smiles spread as your listeners "get" the logic and cleverness of her action.

For another version, see *The Enchanted Orchard and Other Folktales of Central America* by Dorothy Sharp Carter (NY: Harcourt Brace Javanovich, 1973) pp. 83-6.

The Hot Water Test

Africa (Nigeria), page 91

Motif H221.4.1 *Suspected thieves to drink hot water. Tortoise arranges to serve others, giving water time to cool before he drinks. Walks about showing everyone what a big gourdful of water he is taking, cooling it further.*

The miscarriage of justice in this story usually produces animated discussions. African tales sometimes communicate that justice, like life, is imperfect. My bottom line is that the proverb at the story's end justifies the telling.

I initially discovered this story in *Olode The Hunter and Other Tales From Nigeria* by Harold Courlander (NY: Harcourt, Brace & World, 1968) pp. 90-95.

Other Books and Audiocassettes from August House

Thirty-Three Multicultural Tales to Tell
Pleasant DeSpain
Hardback $25.00 / ISBN 0-87483-265-9
Paperback $15.00 / ISBN 0-87483-266-7

Twenty-Two Splendid Tales to Tell,
Volumes One and Two
Pleasant DeSpain
Volume One, paperback $11.95 / ISBN 0-87483-340-X
Volume Two, paperback $11.95 / ISBN 0-87483-341-8

Ready-to-tell Tales
Surefire Stories from America's Favorite Storytellers
Edited by David Holt and Bill Mooney
Hardback $24.95 / ISBN 0-87483-380-9
Paperback $16.95 / ISBN 0-87483-381-7

Favorite Scary Stories of American Children
Richard and Judy Dockrey Young
Hardback $12.95 / ISBN 0-87483-395-7
Paperback $6.95 / ISBN 0-87483-394-9
Audiobook $12.00 / ISBN 0-87483-148-2 (for grades K-3)
Audiobook $12.00 / ISBN 0-87483-175-X (for grades 4-6)

The Southern Bells
Created and Performed by Donald Davis
Audiobook $12.00 / 0-87483-390-6

Telling Your Own Stories
For Family and Classroom Storytelling,
Public Speaking, and Personal Journaling
Donald Davis
Paperback $10.00 / ISBN 0-87483-235-7

Itsy Bitsy Spider's Heroic Climb
and Other Stories
David Novak
Audiobook $12.00 / 0-87483-346-9

The Cookie Girl
Created and Performed by David Novak
Audiobook $12.00 / 0-87483-389-2

Olde Mother Goose
Classic Nursery Rhymes
Accompanied by Traditional Instruments
Performed by the Hubbards
Audiocassette and Booklet $12.95 / 0-87483-213-6

Race with Buffalo
and Other Native American Stories
for Young Readers
Collected by Richard and Judy Dockrey Young
Hardback $19.95 / ISBN 0-87483-343-4
Paperback $9.95 / ISBN 0-87483-342-6

Haunted Bayou
And other Cajun Ghost Stories
J.J. Reneaux
Hardback $18.95 / ISBN 0-87483-384-1
Paperback $9.95 / ISBN 0-87483-385-X

Once Upon a Galaxy
Josepha Sherman
Hardback $19.95 / ISBN 0-87483-386-8
Paperback $11.95 / ISBN 0-87483-387-6

The Animals Could Talk
Aesop's Fables Retold in Song
Heather Forest
Audiocassette and booklet $12.95 / ISBN 0-87483-344-2

August House Publishers, Inc.
P.O. Box 3223
Little Rock, AR 72203
1-800-284-8784